The Fireside

and

Armchair Collections

Volume I

C. E. Shy

inner child press, ltd.

Credits

Author

C. E. Shy

Editor

hülya n. yılmaz, Ph.D.

Cover Graphics & Design

William S. Peters Sr.
inner child press, ltd.

General Information

The Fireside and Armchair Collections, Volume I

C. E. Shy

1st Edition: 2021

Publisher Information:
Inner Child Press International
www.innerchildpress.com

ISBN-13: 978-1-952081-34-7 (inner child press, ltd.)

$ 12.95

Dedicated

to my parents,

Clyde and Esterlee Shy

Table of Contents

Table of Contents . . . *continued*

Preface

The Fireside and Armchair Collections is my first book of flash fiction. This work, a compilation of adventures, has been on my mind for a number of years. It is being offered to the reader with the hope for enjoyment and a ride on the waters of imagination.

The Fireside

and

Armchair Collections

Volume I

C. E. Shy

Airport Chicago

The Fireside and Armchair Collections

Chapter 1

In 1997, I resided in the UAE for 7 or 8 months. I traveled back and forth between Europe, Africa and the Gulf States. Dubai was my main destination. I maintained an office there with a Sudanese friend, who happened to be raised in Egypt. It was very hot there most of the time.

The winter months were perfect. One of the things I liked about being there is that the police didn't single me out. There was no barrier to where I could go. As long as I could afford it, I was okay. Nothing special. The only time that would happen was when you would see an American. They wanted to know how I got there. I had been dealing with crap all my life. I always would try and avoid them. Thank God it was rare. I was going to have to deal with that soon enough.

Chapter 2

My time there was up, and I was headed back to my family who lived in the US. I really wanted to stay in the UAE / Europe / Africa. I had family back in the US; so, I had to go. It turned out the flight was going to land in Chicago. I guess it didn't matter where it landed.

It was going to be the same shit no matter what or where it touched down. True to form, as I stood in the customs line, I watched all the white people clear with no problem. There was a black guy in front of me, and he was catching hell. I could see the hatred in the eyes of the customs agent. The man looked at me and said, 'you see this sick bitch'. He said it without opening his mouth. I acknowledged what he said in the same manner he said it. There was another agent that was standing and watching the exchange between us. He signaled me to an empty stall and told me to go. No inspection. He said, "Welcome home."

The Bus Ride

Chapter 1

Every Monday morning, Ralph took the bus to work. He worked in the mailroom of the company, and had knowledge of computers. There was a problem once with the company's computers. They were about to call for an expert. Ralph heard about it and fixed the problem. He never told anyone he was the one who fixed it. Judy worked for the same company. Judy took the same bus Ralph rode. She worked at the front desk. Judy dressed very well and always smelled of flowers. You could see why she was in charge of the reception desk.

She boarded on the bus two stops after Ralph's stop. They spoke every day; she, with a half-smile, Ralph with a half nod.

Chapter 2

Judy started looking a little different. Ralph no longer smelled the flowers. She never wore the same dress in a week's time. She seemed to be friendly. She sat next to Ralph. She was as soft as cotton. Ralph thought, *Wow, I don't need this*. He was coming out of a separation with his ex-wife. He knew something was wrong with the present situation.

He caught a hint of liquor on her breath. Judy began to talk about her daughter. She was sick, and the doctors didn't know what was wrong with her. Ralph listened and asked what kind of symptoms her daughter was having. Judy was beginning to tear up. She pulled out a tissue and dried her eyes. She went into some detail about her daughter's condition.

Chapter 3

The bus pulled in front of the office. Judy shifted into her job mode. She changed in front of Ralph's eyes. He was amazed. He noticed that she left a small piece of paper on his briefcase with a phone number. It had fallen to the ground.

He reported to his station. As he walked past the front desk, Judy looked as if nothing happened. She glanced at Ralph as he walked by. He thought about Judy's daughter all morning. He didn't want to become Judy's physical relief. He was sure it would be great. He had to figure how he could help her and be unattached.

Then it came to him. There was an herb he felt could turn the girl's condition around. What she had, he thought, was something he heard before. He was going to send the information to Judy. He was up for transfer to another office. He saw where this was headed. He didn't need the emotional connection. Judy was going to have to find someone else.

It was Friday. He posted a letter to her office address with the information. It worked in two of the cases before. He hoped it would work for her daughter. After that day, he never saw her Judy again, even though he wanted to.

The Cigarette Lady

Chapter 1

Tariq lived in a senior citizen building. He was lucky to get the apartment when he did. He was returning from abroad. He had lived in Pakistan for a considerable period of time. He made a living by teaching English and French.

Things started to heat up there, and he felt 27 years was enough. His wife had died. There were very close. It was time to come back to the US.

I asked him once, if things had been different, would he have stayed in Pakistan. He told me it was never his intention to come back. Well, he was back here in the USA.

To be the age he was, he was in very good shape. The apartment was just right for him. It was a one-bedroom with a smaller room that could hold a pullout bed. It was in the back of the building. There was an empty apartment across the hall. It was very peaceful in his flat. Tariq had found a soft place to land.

Chapter 2

After 3 months of peace, he heard people outside his door one morning. When he looked through the peephole, he saw someone was finally moving in across the hall. He wondered what kind of a person it would be. He knew they would be old and most likely set in their ways.

Tariq went back to writing his memoirs. He ran into a friend who introduced him to a publisher. He hadn't seen the friend since high school. When he told him about his life in Pakistan, his friend gave him the number to the publisher and said, the publisher was looking for a story like his.

Chapter 3

That evening as Tariq sat reading and listening to his overseas radio, he smelled cigarette smoke. "Oh no, don't tell me the person smokes!"

He flew into a rage. He opened his door and began to spray the hall with all he had at his disposal. He could hear her choking and coughing. He hoped she would die. This went on for at least 3 months.

He complained to the management. They said, as long as she didn't smoke in the common areas, there was nothing they could do. Then with another stroke of luck, he was told she was run over by a hit-and-run driver and didn't survive. He felt nothing.

Destinations

The Fireside and Armchair Collections

C. E. Shy

Chapter 1

Our pace was different and so were the paths we took, or mistook. In the beginning, we lived close as neighbors. We played together in the playground. At some point in time, we moved on to Jr. High School. We had new friends who joined us. Then we developed different interests and girlfriends. Later, when we got older, I began to be disillusioned with the status quo stuff.

Chapter 2

Our paths grew further apart, but I always considered you a close friend. You were off to college, and I took off to a foreign land. It was the first time in my young life when I felt very relaxed.

It was my first experience with a different kind of human being. I began to write again, free of the side effects of racism. My path swerved widely from all the people I remembered. I was 21, but 41. I had a clear view that would never again be altered. Bullshit wore bells. I could hear it coming before I saw it.

Chapter 3

Time seemed to fly after that. You found your own path to understanding and seeing the demons around you, both black and white.

All those before us and those who were with us had destinations. I can show you their graves where ambitions ended. All destinations – yours and mine, the smart, the blind and the dirt signify the period at the end of this life's line.

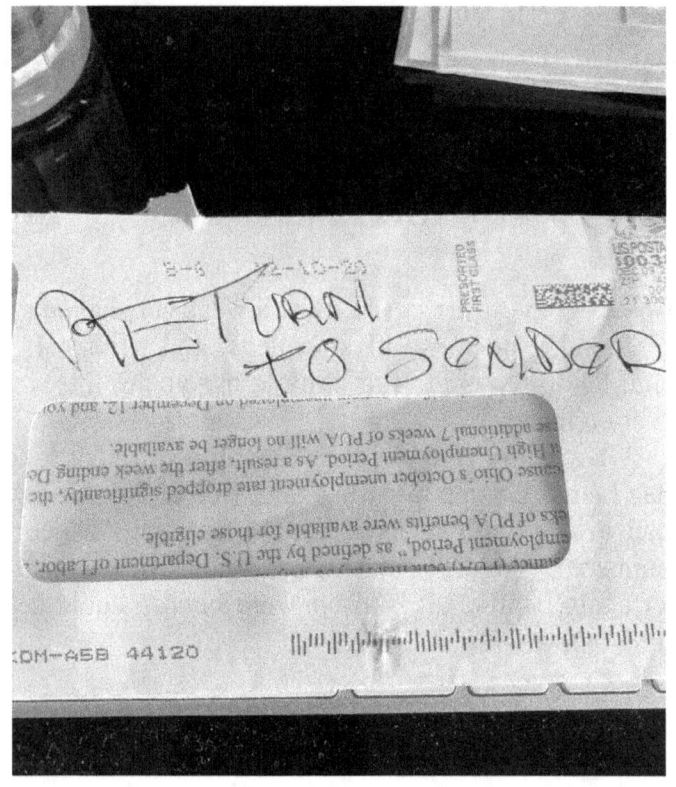

The Mailman's Dilemma

The Fireside and Armchair Collections

Chapter 1

Barry thought it's either too hot or too cold. His attitude had to be, 'if it's too cold for everybody else, it's just right for me.' It was essential to think like that to do his job. He had developed various sayings that helped him survive the trauma of delivering the mail.

Barry had 700 hundred customers on his route. Half of them were in apartment buildings. His day started at the post office in his district.

It began with coffee from the machine that hardly ever worked properly, and the coffee was horrible. The personnel tried different ways to get a good brew. It didn't work. Barry left early to stop at a neighborhood coffee shop to start his day.

Chapter 2

All that week, the weather was very cold. Once he hit the street, he had to walk fast to stay warm, even though he wore warm clothing. Barry was outgoing and got along well with his customers.

There were different kinds of folks he dealt with during the month. There were those who at the first of the month were very friendly. There were those that would not come to the door when they saw him bringing a letter they had to sign.

There was one street that had dogs that waited for his small mail truck to pull up, so they could bark and growl at him. After being pepper-sprayed, they would stay away. On one occasion, a house he delivered to always kept the porch light on. The mail would accumulate for days, then the box would be empty. One day when he was parking, he noticed the police and EMS parked in front of that house.

Chapter 3

When he got out of his truck and started towards the house, a police officer asked him when he saw the person that lived in the house the last time. Barry told the policeman; he never saw who lived there. Then he told him how the letters would be there for days before someone would empty the box.

Later that day, he heard that an old lady lived at that address. She was an invalid. There were dire circumstances. The lady owned dogs. She was not able to feed them when she became ill. The dogs ate her. Barry got sick and had to call off early. That was only one of the many houses with many stories left to tell.

Change of Mind

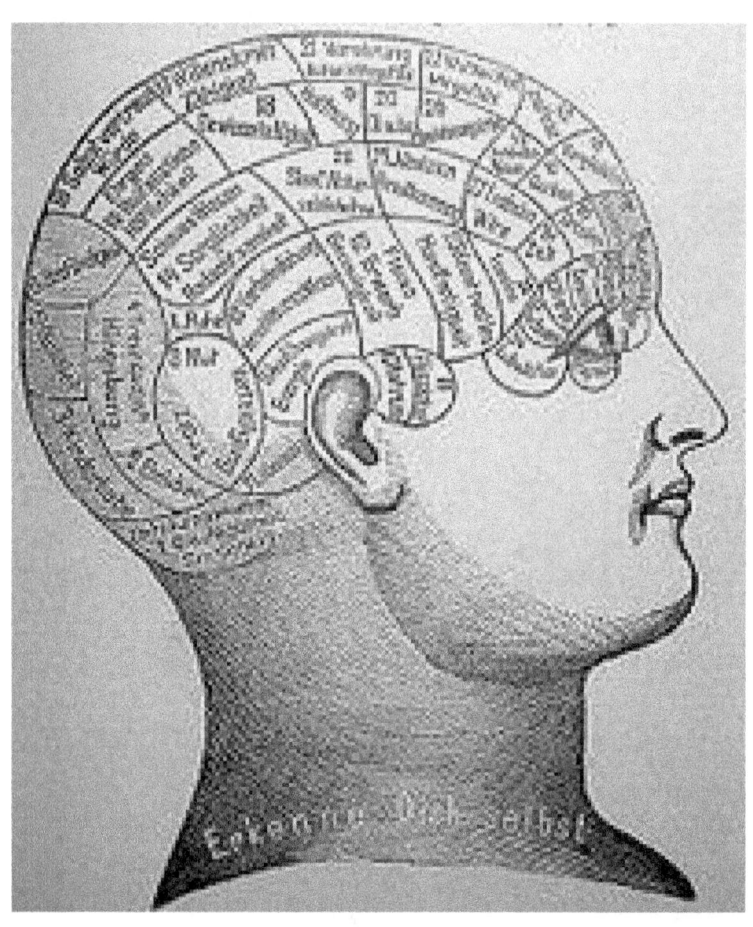

Chapter 1

This started out as a poem. As I thought about it for a minute, I changed my mind two or three times. I think it was the light she saw in me and on me that made her question my intentions. She wanted to know where my stare was headed. I asked her if I really needed to explain what was plainly there. She told me her math couldn't add it up. I asked her to sit, so that I could try to make her understand the things she couldn't hear.

Chapter 2

I told her a book was in the making and she was making me write it.

I sat and she sat. We were by the sea. I began to tell her where my words came from. I said, if she listened long enough, they would be her words too. I was opening up the bliss thing. She mentioned she heard some of what I was saying, but she woke up so the dream could finish.

Chapter 3

She told me; she was on water-fast. That's why she could keep up somewhat. I told her I was just visiting, and at some point, I had to go back.

She wanted to know: "Back to where? Are there more people like you there?" "Not a whole lot". She said there weren't any like me here. So, we left when our ship came in.

New

The Fireside and Armchair Collections

C. E. Shy

Chapter 1

I kept fooling around with her. Then one day, she called my bluff. I tried to put my best look forth. I mean, I wanted it to seem like I could handle whatever was to happen next.

I may have gone too far to say I was just playing. I talked too harshly. I wish I hadn't started this. I'm in it now.

The lady was in her 40s. She was finished with the insecurities of her 30s. I had been in a lot of things that challenged me – events I couldn't walk away from and that I had to finish.

She was educated in the ways of the street. She had a degree from an Ivy League college. She owned a coffee shop in a newly developed area. I was invited there for whatever I drank.

Chapter 2

When I entered, she raised her hand and I went over to where she sat. She leaned over, and we touched lightly – cheek to cheek. The first thing she asked was, "what does Sifer mean?" I told her it meant zero in Arabic. "Is that your last name?" she wanted to know. "Yes", I said.

I ordered black tea and she did the same. The waiter asked if I wanted sugar or some other sweetener. I said, zero. She laughed out loud. She was not insecure.

"I know you know my name", she said. I asked if I could call her anything. She laughed and said, "I'm not disappointed."

I was not wasting my time.

She responded, "Okay, as long as you know my name." I told her I wanted to know what God called her and I asked if she knew. She got up and said, "We can't finish this conversation here."

She said there was another place she had in mind. When we arrived, the topic changed and things intensified.

That was the way my wife was. Then she died. It was 20 years ago today. It all still feels like new to me.

No Sirens Tonight

C. E. Shy

Chapter 1

I talked to a neighbor when I came back from a road trip. It was late in the evening – actually, close to midnight. He was an elderly man. He was about 90 years old. As I walked up the steps to the door, he spoke to me and said, "I have been sitting out here on this porch most of the night. I have not heard one siren all night." I replied: "That is truly amazing. Usually, you can count on hearing them all the time."

Chapter 2

He told me for about the thirtieth time how he was raised in the country and could hear the crickets all night long and see the stars. I was tired. I had just driven 150 miles nonstop. He lived with his wife who was close to his age. I listened to him, until he said," Son, go on and get some rest. You look tired." I thanked him. I asked him to say hello to his wife for me. She was a master cook. I wanted to make sure she knew I asked about her.

Chapter 3

I had not eaten. I refused to eat the crap at the rest stops along the road. In fact, I had some leftover chicken loaf from my neighbor. She made it for me two days ago. I didn't use the microwave a lot, but that night I did. I took a shower and tried to go to sleep. I must have slept for a couple of hours. I was awakened by, of all things, a siren. I smiled and thought, there goes my neighbor's silent night.

Chapter 4

When I woke up the next morning, there was a knock on my door. It was Mrs. Smith. She informed me that her husband had passed away during the night on the way to the hospital. She asked me to take her to the funeral home to make the necessary arrangements. That broke my heart.

I was happy that I had listened to Mr. Smith that night. You never know.

On My Heels

C. E. Shy

Chapter 1

Realizing my vulnerabilities, I stay away – most of the time. God knows, I don't want to. What may please me, may not please Him. My pleasure is only temporary. I aim for the longer bliss.

In certain situations, I would be powerless. I would be wrong for being there. Whatever collective moments of bliss I enjoyed would be a deficit. Time wasted in the face of the greatness ahead . . .

As I thumb through the pages of my memory, I realize there are forgotten things attached to those lost memories. There were added moments of bliss, the highs and lows of passion. They are written somewhere. I hope when confronted with them, if ever; they will be washed away from the Master Books records.

Chapter 2

As I stared across the room, I was hoping that she wouldn't look up and smile at me. I hoped her vibration would not attract me. I would only lose the game in which she is the master. So, I drank my coffee and left in a hurry. It was just in time, because her eyes followed me out the door. They were beckoning me to return. I began to walk faster and faster. I remote-started my car. I could sense the temptation in my heels. I opened the door, put in on drive and then said to myself, 'I can't go back there anymore.'

2:54 📶 📶 🔋

‹ The Moon   **Moon Data**   2:54 PM

Moonset	5:30 AM
Moonrise	3:13 PM
Azimuth	57° 57' 45"
Altitude	-3° 04' 57"
Distance	401 726 km
Angular Diameter	0° 29' 44"
Ecliptic Longitude	70° 09' 20"
Ecliptic Latitude	0° 48' 07"
Obliquity Of The Ecliptic	23° 26' 11"
Local Sidereal Time	20h 55m 24s
Right Ascension	4h 34m 36s
Declination	21° 10' 34"

Waxing Gibbous   94.8%

Full Moon
December 29

New Moon
January 12

Day 13   Day 14

Overnight

Chapter 1

On my way to Paris, I knew that being there overnight wasn't going to be enough time. I was contracted for a gig that was being held at the Eiffel Tower. I was traveling with a drummer named Hasan. We hadn't played together in years.

It was Thursday morning when we left JFK. Hasan sat with his practice pad, going through his progressions. I used my handgrip, making sure my fingers would be up to the task.

Chapter 2

I couldn't help thinking about my previous stay in Paris. It had been years since I last saw it. I liked everything about the place. I still could speak French. I had friends in Paris and Nice. I stayed in touch with them. They would be traveling to see the show.

This was the first trip to Paris for Hasan. His concern was about the ladies and French pastries. He wasn't going to be there long enough to get a feel of the city of lights. He had a gig in Denmark and was leaving Saturday noon.

Chapter 3

I was very surprised to see two of my old friends there to greet me, Daniel and his wife Adalene. They were the principal managers of the Chanel fashion show. It is the most important event in the world of fashion. Top models and designers from everywhere compete to be in that show.

We hugged each other. I introduced them to Hasan. They dropped us off at our hotel. We were invited to a rehearsal for the fashion show that evening. After the rehearsal, Hasan said he might cancel his gig in Denmark. Of course, he was kidding.

Chapter 4

There was a large crowd that gathered for the gig. The acoustics were excellent. We played for 2 hours. We were a quintet. The audience was very receptive.

After the performance, Hasan shook my hands and gave me a big hug. He took off with a young lady who had picked him up. That was not unusual behavior for musicians. Daniel and his wife had planned a dinner at the Ritz Carlton. We arrived there at 9:45 PM. The first person I saw was an ex-pat. He was the house piano player, Bobby Few. We had played together in the U.S. He saw me, smiled, and then told the people at the restaurant he was dedicating a song to an old friend. The song was called "In Walked Bud."

We were seated. I casually looked around the room. Sitting at a table alone was the first lady I had connected with during my first stay in Paris. She recognized me. I excused myself from my friends' table, went over to her, and asked if she was . . . Before I could finish my sentence, she said, "Yes." "May I sit?" When I glanced at my friends, they were smiling. It was a set-up. I never again left France.

Passages

C. E. Shy

Chapter 1

I loved you for an extended period of time. I had no idea that 3000 years could pass so fast.

We met first in the desert, when wind-blown stones were flying behind the pyramids. As time went by, we found ourselves in places that made us separate from one another, having us search for each other.

We were always able to connect. When Rome burned, we escaped the fire. The news reached us on the banks of the Nile. The decree was to take us back in time.

Chapter 2

As the wind swirled, we were locked in an embrace that nearly took our breath away. We woke up in Bagdad.

Our children were scholars. They helped to name the stars to chart the skies. The idea that someone would copy those names had never entered our minds. We found an ally in the time; one that would share its secrets with us. It informed us that it was instructed to be kind. It – time was to make the passage smooth for you and me.

Chapter 3

Today, we celebrate our time here in this phase of our existence. We have been able to see and be involved in the development of the world. We watched the destruction of it as well. There are no regrets for what has happened with us. I think I can also speak for you on this matter. Our children have been good for the world, and their children have maintained the ideas established by us.

She, my companion, just told me that we have an appointment with the decree. On the other side of time, there is no time.

• • •

Relief

C. E. Shy

Chapter 1

I had my first airplane ride in February 1963. I was going to Stockholm, Sweden. Icelandic Airlines or Airways was the carrier. At this moment, the name escapes me. I remember the weather being very cold and snowy. The name of the airport was at the time Idlewild International Airport.

The plane was a turbo prop. I was assigned a seat in the back of the plane. It being my first trip over the Atlantic, I had no idea that it wasn't the best seat in the house. The weather turned so terrible that the flight had to be cancelled. The passengers were shuttled to hotels on Long Island.

Chapter 2

Upon our arrival at the hotel, we were directed to the front desk in order to be assigned our rooms for the night. I was the only African American man on the flight. There was a black lady with a baby. Her husband was in military service in Germany. The final destination of the flight was going to be Frankfurt.

This incident was my first taste of outright racism. I asked for the bar area. They were going to call me when they had a room for me. Okay, this was the real America I was getting a real close-up look at. I couldn't help but think that I was leaving all of this behind me. 'Maybe', I wondered, 'the whole world was like this.'

Chapter 3

When I returned to the front desk, I couldn't see any of the passengers there. Many of them were in the bar talking about the delays and a variety of subjects. On that trip, there were exchange students going to a university in Copenhagen.

As I stood at the desk waiting for the receptionist, one of the students approached me and asked if I was given a room. I told him, "not yet". When the employee was back at his station, the student asked him why I did not have a room yet. He began to stutter and said that they were working on it.

The student told him to put me in the room with him and some other students. His name was Eddie. He told the jerk behind the desk who his father was and that he was going to call him, if the requested arrangement was not made right away. The task was completed immediately.

The next morning, we were loaded on a bus and taken to the airport to catch our flight. I thanked Eddie for his help. He smiled and said, "no problem."

Remarkable Friends

The Fireside and Armchair Collections

C. E. Shy

Chapter 1

It was a Saturday evening in late July. A friend, Y, was visiting his daughter in a rather unsavory part of the city. That evening, there was a gang initiation taking place in that part of the town. He was in the projects.

While on the way to his daughter's apartment, he was approached by a young guy who asked him for money. After he told the guy he had none, he walked away. All of a sudden, he felt a sharp pain in his back. He realized that he had been shot. Then he was hit again. He was shot a total of 6 times. Somehow, he was able to turn on his side as the guy was running away and get off enough rounds to kill him.

Those 6 shots he sustained made it the 19th time he had been shot. He is still around today. If you were to see him, you could never imagine that happened.

Chapter 2

My friend K was just a little different. He had been shot nine times – "all by accident," he claims. The first time was at a barbershop. The owner of the shop sold guns. K was sitting in the barber chair when one of the guns went off and hit him in the leg, right below his knee.

The next time it happened, he was in a gambling joint, when two of the patrons got into an argument. As one of them was trying to get away, the other one shot at him and the bullet bounced off the door and hit K in the shoulder. K told me three years passed before he was shot again.

This time, it was on New Year's Eve. He was sitting on his back porch when a bullet hit him in the foot. Another time, he got caught in a crossfire on his way from the doctor's office. He was hit twice then. He says, he can't remember where he was the next time it happened; he said he was too drunk.

K woke up in the hospital and he had a cast on his forearm. He always wound up in the same hospital. The doctors and nurses knew him well. The guy is still around. Every time you ask how he is doing, his answer is always the same: "I'm sick, man!"

Rich

C. E. Shy

Chapter 1

Claude was a very good athlete. He was also confident about what he could accomplish in life. He was 17 years old at the time. He told a classmate that he would be wealthy by the time he was 29 years old.

He was not a person who was very interested in academics. Claude never studied much, and his grades reflected that. The thing that kept him in school was sports. He was a 3-letter-man. He would look at his geography book and go to the library to write stories. He was going to travel to India when he graduated from high school.

Chapter 2

By this time, Claude became aware that getting wealthy in America wasn't going to be easy. He was starting to wish he remained in Europe. He had something to compare to where he was born. America was a racist hellhole.

Many of the kids Claude grew up with had gone completely different directions. Most of his black classmates were experiencing the same racist demons. He began to react to racism by joining groups of black men and women who were race-conscious.

One day, he ran into the white classmate he had told he was going to rich by the time he was 29. The first thing that classmate asked him was, "Are you rich yet, Claude?" He knew from the very beginning that Claude wasn't going to have an easy time fulfilling his dream in America. The classmate was by then an alcoholic.

Chapter 3

Years passed before Claude was able to connect with former classmates. Every single one of them told him about their struggles with racism. Many of them said they changed their dreams when they were overwhelmed by it.

They said they were to going to give their children a heads-up through their experiences so they wouldn't get blindsided like we were as kids. Our parents aimed for integration, which was the biggest mistake ever made by our people. They agreed.

As time passed, Claude became more convinced that the struggle was about good against evil. That was the higher knowledge he achieved through his experiences. Self-contentment was the wealth he gained.

Separation

C. E. Shy

Chapter 1

Terry was having trouble separating his music and the way he wrote. The voice he heard when playing his instrument was different than the one that spoke when he wrote.

When he practiced, he would change the locations where he practiced. Terry would go to another place to write. He felt the different atmospheres would bring something new.

He knew he wasn't one-dimensional in his expressions. There were many musicians who tried to bridge the gap between writing words and writing notes. They would try their hand at various modes of artistic endeavors. Very few could fulfill an equal expression to their satisfaction. Eventually, they would do one or the other.

Chapter 2

During a gig he played with a Chinese and Afro-Cuban group, he made the connection. The next day, he sat in his library and wrote his first musical play. It was called, "Touch and Go". He finally bridged the two.

The vibrations of the two cultures helped him to distinguish the voices. He was able keep his personal thoughts away from his artistic expression. The place he lived was not given to artistic expression. It wasn't a place that would accommodate everyone.

Due to the rust belt, meat and potatoes mindset, Terry realized he would have to leave that city in order to explore and develop his potential as a writer and musician.

As fate would have it, he was afforded an opportunity in Paris, France to work at his craft. He never returned to the U.S.

Shoes

Chapter 1

Willie tried his best to find some blue suede shoes. He wanted to make them come alive from the record album. There were some around, but they didn't look like the one the "king" wore.

What made him angry was that his little sister loved Chuck Berry. He remembered when he was a kid, his father shot up his collection of the "king's" records. His father had said, the cat copied black dudes and made millions.

His dad was a staunch blues guy. The only record that survived was the blue suede shoes 45 rpm. He still hid it, just in case his dad came back, found it and shot it up too. Willie's Pop was dead. The very thought of what had happened back then made him paranoid.

Chapter 2

Willie was 55 years old and he couldn't let go of his life in the projects. He would still go down there and look at the place where he grew up. It was no longer standing. He would look up at where he thought his old bedroom would have been located.

The swing set was there, but the merry-go-round was gone. So were the bushes where he kissed his first girlfriend. He never lingered there for long. The neighborhood was not the same as it was before. It had become a dangerous place.

One day, Willie got some bad news. The projects were going to be torn down. He was depressed for a month. The only thing that brought him out of his depression was his cousin, who knew of his quest, and found some blue suede shoes on line. Willie knew his mother would be happy for him, but his Pop . . .

Shopping

C. E. Shy

Chapter 1

One Christmas season, I was at work on the railroad. Being the major foreman of the tie gang, it was my responsibility to walk the line and check on the work being done. There were 100 men in the gang with 5 regular foremen. Some of them needed more supervision than others.

There were some guys that would share some things in their life and would ask for advice. You could give advice to some. There was a particular conversation I recall more than any of them. It was a couple of days before Xmas. For the sake of the person's privacy, I'll call him "Frank".

Chapter 2

As I walked by the men and gave them my season's greetings, Frank stopped me and said, he wanted to tell me how proud he was of his wife. He was smiling and started telling me the most amazing story.

Frank told me; his wife had all the Xmas shopping done. The thing he was most proud of was that his wife had stolen all the gifts, along with the tree and even all the wrapping paper. I stood there in disbelief.

He looked up at me and stopped smiling. I guess, he felt that I didn't understand. I asked him if he didn't see anything wrong with that. Frank then asked me something I found to be mind-blowing. 'If the Grinch could steal Xmas, what was wrong with his wife doing it?' He was serious. Every time Xmas comes around, I think of that conversation.

Space Travel

The Fireside and Armchair Collections

C. E. Shy

Chapter 1

During most of the times we meet, there is a space between us. I would like very much to close the gap. Mentally, it does not exist. We turn the pages at the same time. I see what you see. You control that space. How can I convince you to move closer? Are you aware that it's there?

Chapter 2

Sometimes, I wish he would stand a little closer. Hopefully, like minds think alike. When he passes the documents, they have the fragrance of musk. Just how strong is he? Should I violate his space? I was never taught how to deal with this in graduate school. It never came with my MBA.

Chapter 3

Her amber eyes avoid mine as we dance around an issue. She used to wear Jimmy Choo, but now she wears nothing. The rumors are, she wears a scar from a former situation. Sometimes, I wait in my car hoping that her car won't start. That might close the space between us.

At the company dinner, she entered the room and introduced her intended guest. Someone else had filled the space between her and me. I happen to think, I was too old for her anyway.

I had to come up with something.

The Designer

The Fireside and Armchair Collections

Chapter 1

Wednesday morning, I received a call from Don who is a friend and a business associate. I hadn't talked with him for a few months. After a transaction we were working on fell through, we took a break. He was excited about something. He began telling about a friend of his. She was a designer and had some success locally and nationally. Don wanted to know if I had any contacts in Paris. He knew I lived there for some time. He remembered me telling him about a big fashion show I had attended.

Chapter 2

I asked him to slow down a little. I wasn't able to get a word in edgewise. My first question to him was, "Does the lady have any money?" Next, "Where does she live?" I told him to put what they have in an email to me and, if there were any samples, to send them to me. I told him I was in Atlanta and would be there for another 2 weeks. He was surprised. He said the lady was in Atlanta and on the phone with him.

"Thanks for letting me know!"

"Sorry, Ali."

At that moment, the lady spoke: "Don, I can take this from here."

Chapter 3

She introduced herself. "My name is Susan Smith." We exchanged greetings.

Don thanked me for my time. My thought was, he must know something I don't know. I didn't make any commitment. Susan asked me where I was located in Atlanta. She could bring all the items I inquired about to my location. I gave her my hotel and my suite's number. She said, she was excited about the project and that she would be grateful if I could help.

Chapter 4

When she arrived at the hotel, I was in the lobby. I thought, 'this couldn't be her'. I knew her from social media. We were exchanging posts for more than a year. She was absolutely beautiful! I stepped in front of her and asked was she there to meet a person about . . . Before I finished my sentence, she said, "I know you." We both laughed. I thought about how many times I flirted with her and she returned it on more than a few occasions. Now, we were together in the lobby of that hotel. Every time we glanced at each other, we smiled. She wrapped her arm around me, then took my arm and put it around her. The elevator door was opening as we approached. We were on our way to my suite.

The Maid Service

C. E. Shy

Chapter 1

Jack Kay hired a maid service. He lived in a large house just on the outskirts of the city. Jack was far too busy to do any cleaning around the house. There were 5 bedrooms, a large kitchen, a formal dining room and a living room overlooking a small lake. There were five and a half bathrooms with a sauna in two of them.

There was a multi-car garage with a small office on top of it all. There was a bathroom in the heated garage with a shower. In the basement of the house was an in-law suite. Jack's friend conducted interviews with prospective maids that would occupy that suite.

Rukya, Jack's friend, interviewed 14 maids before she recommended one of them to him. The woman was fifty years old, very stable and had good references from the embassy. She was Russian. She migrated to the U.S. when she was 21 years old.

Chapter 2

Jack hired her on Rukya's word. He barely saw her or heard her in the house. He was very pleased with her work. She also took care of a small garden that produced fresh herbs and tomatoes. Rukya was from Bosnia. She spent half of the year in the U.S. and the rest in Bosnia with her family.

Jack's doctor told him, he was working too hard and he needed to take some time off. His maid Korvia had no idea that he was going to work part-time out of his home.

Jack was going to be mostly relaxing. As he was sitting by the lake, a woman came from the back of the garage, wearing a thong and no top. His eyes were opened as wide as possible. At first, she didn't see him, until he shouted at her, "Who are you and what the hell are you doing here?" She tried to cover herself . . . unsuccessfully.

Chapter 3

She was absolutely gorgeous! Jack's anger and surprise turned into lust and passion. She saw it in his eyes and she relaxed. She told him that she's Korvia's cousin and just arrived in the U.S. He couldn't keep his eyes off her. He asked her name. She said her friends call her Linenkiva. All he could think about was how he was going to get her into his bed. He asked her, if she was going to be staying with Korvia.

Before she could reply, he said it was ok if she did. Jack took of his sports jacket and draped it around her. She ran to the house with Jack's eyes following her every step of the way.

Chapter 4

It didn't take Jack long before she was in his bed and was staying with him in the house. She made him feel young. He knew, he would not see Rukya for at least 5 months. He put it out of his mind.

One Sunday morning, there was a knock on his door. He saw through his security camera "FBI" on the jackets of six agents. He recognized one of them. He opened the door. The one he knew spoke to him: "Hi, Jack." "Hey, Tom, what's going on?" The senior agent then spoke: "We are here to arrest Ludmila Rajnoff." "Who?" Jack asked. Tom said, "Yeah, Jack. She is a spy and her friend Korvia is one too."

Jack had to sit down. Tom said, "We had to bug your house. We know you had nothing to do with it. Oh, by the way, Rukya works for us." Tom tried to console Jack by telling him that on many occasions he had wished he had been Jack. The two women were in custody, and theirs was a courtesy visit.

Jack grabbed a bottle of vodka and Ludmilla's picture and drank several rounds before passing out in his living room.

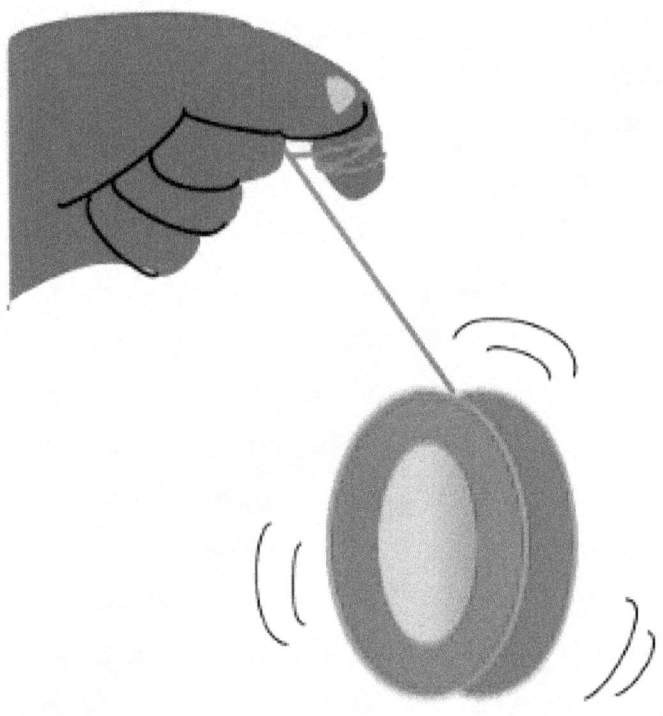

The Yoyo-ist

C. E. Shy

Chapter 1

Clark thought he had gotten away from the string that was attached to his life. It was just a longer string. He was a Yoyo-ist. His older brother had a heck of a time trying to convince him of that fact. Sometimes it's difficult to tell a smart person something, because they usually talk when you're talking.

Clark kept saying, he didn't trust in a particular belief system, an organized way of life. He preferred his unorganized way of life. His brother told him that was a religion. It was his religion. That nobody should interfere with his beliefs. People who choose a way of life other than Clark's should not offend Clark.

Chapter 2

His uncle John reminded Clark that in his religion adultery was okay, fornication was okay, and being intoxicated was a part of his way of life. His religion allowed all the things mentioned. There were no rules. Things changed as he needed them to. His way of life was similar to the religion of Himalism.

The thing he admired so much about his way of life was that he could pray if he wanted to or not, because God knew what was in his heart. The good thing about Clark was that he was really a good guy. He was learning that the strings were still attached no matter how far the Yoyo spun.

What Did You Say?
I Can't Hear You!

C. E. Shy

Chapter 1

It was the wine that made me smile a little bit. It didn't take much to make me stagger. I was still a long way from being high. I sat on a high stool and picked up my bow. I started strumming my bass. I ignored most of the notes on the page and relied on the ones in my head. I played the saxophones' solo, while holding the bottom line. The critics said, I played criminal music and slick stuff that rolled from between the strings of my sax.

Chapter 2

The band was playing things; it was rough for the people to understand. Our sounds broke the jukebox. The music went outside before anyone could stop it.

A lady in the club started crying. The claim was, the music was hurting her feelings. I had dealt with her kind. She was looking to sue.

A poet began to recite a poem called "Chang A Lang." Then a soprano started to sing. The chandelier broke and the glass was in A sharp.

Chapter 3

The drummer was out there. He was on his own. The piano player was getting drunk. I forgot that I left the rosin in my car. It was parked too far. I dropped the bow and picked my way through the rest of the jam. The poet recited a poem he just wrote; he called it, "I Do Dat Sometime." We played that jam for one hour. The poet never stopped. He kept on rapping. It was a little after the closing hour. It was then when the cops came in.

Chapter 4

They told the owner, "Don't close now." They were patting their feet and tapping clubs on the bar. Everybody was caught in the groove. The only way the night ended was when the drummer broke all his sticks, the piano player fell on the floor, and the soprano started sounding baritone. The poet lost his voice. I had drunk up all the rest of the wine. The sun was up. Now, the owner could close the joint down.

Yawning

C. E. Shy

Chapter 1

I sit on the side of the bed yawning. With the back of my left hand, I cover my mouth. Somebody told me that was the way you do it. I contemplate how I will dodge under miners until another day dawns. When I look out the window, I see the speculators are surrounding me. I thought I saw a pussycat. It was just an aberration of a human being. There is more to fear from what you can see than what you can't.

Chapter 2

I know there is another guy sitting on the side of his bed yawning, trying to figure out how he is going to screw me this morning. As his mind flounders in the fog, he bends down to kiss the dog. He can't wait to get to my side of town so he can see how much hell he can lay down. When he goes home after work, he's like a hero to his butcher, his baker and the cold beer-maker. Most of the time you see him on your side of town, there is no benefit to you or me by him being around. He carries the Holy Grail in his lunch pail. His kids did what his daddy did.

Chapter 3

There was somebody else who woke up this morning yawning. He started off by asking his God to forgive the Klan, to wash the blood off their hands. He asked him to forgive the demons that hung his dad, burned down his house and took his land, raped his wife, killed his mule, and blew up his kid's school. He wanted forgiveness for all the slave-owners. He wanted God to punish the black guy next door for stepping on his grass.

Zero Cool

C. E. Shy

Chapter 1

I did my part, and everything was cool. At first, when the call came in, I was busy doing something else. I was into me. I had no plans that day, and that was cool. It was midday and I was midway of being cool all day. My friend called and said, he was stranded and he was sick. I almost blew my cool. Then I thought, 'how would I feel if was sick and there wasn't anyone to come and get me?' I told him, if he didn't get a ride in 15 minutes, to call me back. In the meantime, I got dressed and headed out the door to get him.

Chapter 2

It was rush hour; so, the traffic was thick, but we listened to Coltrane all the way to his spot. The traffic didn't even matter. When we pulled in front of his house, he remarked how tired he was and thanked me. It took him a little effort to get out of the car. He was the guy that came up with money to give me to get a car 10 years earlier. It would have been less than cool not to pick him up and take him home.

The Fireside and Armchair Collections

Epilogue

About the Author

C. E. Shy has been writing since the seventh grade. He continued writing through high school, until he became more involved in sports. After his graduation, he worked at the White Motors Company where he wrote for the company's newspaper. He started a column called: "The Poet's Corner." That was his first published work.

With a one-way ticket, he moved to Sweden. He met a Swedish photographer and started writing narratives for some of the photographs which were sold to newspapers and magazines.

After returning to the US, he joined a poetry workshop that was run by Russell Atkins and Norman Jordan from 1966 to 1968. He stopped writing for years, then started to write again in the late 90s, crafting novellas, flash fiction and poetry. He joined a writing workshop in Cleveland, Ohio in 2011 to hone his writing skills.

Other Books

and

Other Works

by the

Author

Come with Me. Urban Fantasy Novel (Inner Child Press International: August 31, 2020)

The Substitute. Romance Novel (Inner Child Press International: July 15, 2020)

Celebrating 50: The Legacy of the Muntu poets of Cleveland by K (February 18, 2018) ~ Poetic Prose

"The Pot!": Poetic Reflections of the Glenville Riots 1968 Cleveland, Ohio (February 18, 2018) ~ Poetry

Mixed Emotions (January 3, 2017) ~ Poetry

Five Minutes Past Midnight (January 29, 2017) ~ Novel

Pens and Needles (January 29, 2017) ~ Poetry

Mr. Gentleman. Nomenclature (February 2, 2017) ~ Audio CD

Sketchings (February 19, 2017) ~ Poetry

PTSD Poems That Say Dream (March 14, 2017)

Traveling in the Light (March 21, 2017) ~ Poetry

Transparent-S (April 24, 2017) ~ Poetry

Tuned In (April 24, 2017) ~ Poetry

More Questions Than Answers (June 1, 2017) ~ Poetry

Gray Area (June 1, 2017) ~ Poetry

Balance (June 27, 2017) ~ Poetry

If I Only Could . . . (August 1, 2017) ~ Poetry

Zero at the End of the Rainbow (August 31, 2017) ~ Poetry

Miles to Go While I Weep (September 26, 2017) ~ Poetry

Signs and Signals (October 7, 2017) ~ Poetry

Watch Out (October 24, 2017) ~ Poetry

A Knock on the Door (October 24, 2017) ~ Poetry

Chapter Z (October 29, 2017) ~ Poetry

The Muntu Poets of Cleveland by Russell Atkins (January 8, 2016) ~ Anthology

The Long and the Short of it: Armchair Chronicles. Volume I, II and III (January 28, 2016) ~ A Short Story Collection

The House (January 28, 2016) ~ Novel

Me and Maysun (February 28, 2016) ~ A Collection of Literary Works

Approaching the Ninth Dimension (April 10, 2016) ~ Poetic Prose

Deliver Me from Unconsciousness (June 7, 2016) ~ Poetic Prose

The Visit (June 12, 2016) ~ Novel

The Door at the End of the Hall (August 22, 2016) ~ Poetry

Point Blank! Eclections 4 (September 19, 2016) ~ Poetry

No U Turns ONE WAY! (October 4, 2016) ~ Poetic Prose

The Glimpse: A Remote View (November 7, 2016) ~ Poetry

Cyber Man (November 9, 2016) ~ Novel

A Frayed (December 11, 2016) ~ Poetry

Straight Up! Compilation 1 (December 30, 2016)
> A collection of poems written by the original members of the Muntu Poets of Cleveland with musical accompaniment

Ain't No Change! Compilation 2 (December 30, 2016)
> A collection of poems written by the original members of the Muntu Poets of Cleveland with musical accompaniment

Time Share (March 20, 2015) ~ Novel

Substitutions (March 20 2015) ~ Novel

Eclections 2: Words in the Wind (March 20, 2015) ~ Poetry and Prose

Eclections 3. Words in My Window (April 27, 2015) ~ Poetry and Prose

Powhims and Proz October 30, 2015 Poetry and Prose

Inner Child Press

Inner Child Press is a publishing company founded and operated by writers. Our personal publishing experiences provide us an intimate understanding of the sometimes-daunting challenges writers, new and seasoned may face in the business of publishing and marketing their creative "Written Work".

For more information:
Inner Child Press

www.innerchildpress.com

intouch@innerchildpress.com

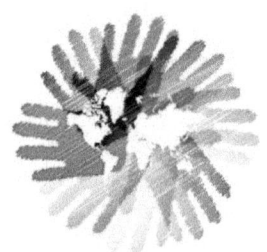

Inner Child Press International

'building bridges of cultural understanding'

202 Wiltree Court, State College, Pennsylvania 16801

www.ingramcontent.com/pod-product-compliance
Lightning Source LLC
Chambersburg PA
CBHW060752180626
46818CB00002B/549